All These Things

Susie Poole

Text and illustrations © 2014 Susie Poole.
Published in 2017 by B&H Publishing Group,
Nashville, Tennessee
ISBN: 978-1-4627-4514-2
Dewey Decimal Classification: CE
Subject Heading: LOVE \ KIND
All rights reserved. Printed in Shenzhen, Guangdong, China.
1 2 3 4 5 6 7 8 · 21 20 19 18 17

B&H KIDS

Nashville, Tennessee

What is
Love?

Kisses and cuddles?

Hugs and squeezes?

Love **is** these things.

But it's **kindness** too.

And learning to **wait** our turn.

It's being grateful

for the things we are given.

And **looking out** for those that are small.

It's taking a
deep breath and
counting to five
when we feel
mad!

Love is saying
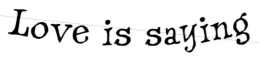
"**no**"
to **bad**
things.

And
"**yes**"

to good things.

Love lets others have a turn,

and hopes they will do **well**.

And when you want to give up...

Love keeps
on going...

Love is
all these things.